BY J. POWELL

ILLUSTRATED BY PAUL SAVAGE
COVER ILLUSTRATED BY MARCUS SMITH

Librarian Reviewer
Marci Peschke
Librarian, Dallas Independent School District
MA Education Reading Specialist, Stephen F. Austin State University
Learning Resources Endorsement, Texas Women's University

Reading Consultant
Mary Evenson
Middle School Teacher, Edina Public Schools, MN
MA in Education, University of Minnesota

STONE ARCH BOOKS
Minneapolis   San Diego

First published in the United States in 2008
by Stone Arch Books
151 Good Counsel Drive, P.O. Box 669
Mankato, Minnesota 56002
www.stonearchbooks.com

Originally published in Great Britain in 2006
by Badger Publishing Ltd.

Library of Congress Cataloging-in-Publication Data
Powell, Jillian.
    [Rollercoaster]
    Roller Coaster / by J. Powell; illustrated by Paul Savage.
    p. cm. (Keystone Books)
    Summary: When three friends who are too young to ride the
gigantic Devil Dipper roller coaster sneak on after the amusement park
has closed, it turns out to be an even scarier ride than they expected.
    ISBN-13: 978-1-59889-850-7 (library binding)
    ISBN-10: 1-59889-850-7 (library binding)
    ISBN-13: 978-1-59889-902-3 (paperback)
    ISBN-10: 1-59889-902-3 (paperback)
    [1. Roller coasters—Fiction. 2. Amusement parks—Fiction.
3. Horror stories.] I. Savage, Paul, 1971– ill. II. Title.
PZ7.P87755Ro 2008
[Fic]—dc22   2007003018

1 2 3 4 5 6 12 11 10 09 08 07

Printed in the United States of America

TABLE OF CONTENTS

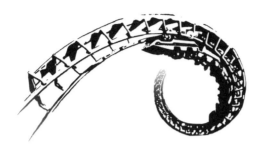

Chapter 1

SORRY, GUYS

There it was. It was a crazy, huge loop of steel. In the middle was a big wheel between two steel spikes.

"Is that cool, or what?" Gus said.

"It is really cool," Ricky and Sam agreed.

Gus read the sign. "From zero to seventy-five miles per hour in two seconds. Each seat spins all the way around!"

"The gravity is so strong you almost pass out if you are sitting in the back seats," Gus told them.

"I heard it's like flying in an F-16 fighter jet," Sam said.

The three of them stood looking up at the steel monster. Then they looked at each other.

"Ready?" Gus said. They joined the line waiting for a ride on the Devil Dipper.

It was a long wait. The line snaked around for what seemed like miles.

Finally, the three boys reached the front of the long line.

The man who was taking tickets at the gate held out his arm. "Sorry, guys, I can't let you on the ride today."

"What?" Gus said. He thought that the man must have been joking.

"You guys are under fourteen," the man said.

He pointed to a sign.

The sign read, "All children under fourteen must be accompanied by an adult."

"Yeah, well, I'm their dad," Ricky joked, pointing at Gus and Sam. "I just look really young."

"And I'm the king of England," the man said. "But you're still not getting on this ride."

People started to push in front of them. The man waved them aside.

"Oh, that's just great," Gus said. "We save up for a month and now we can't even get on the ride."

"That's what he thinks," Ricky said. "Listen. I have an idea."

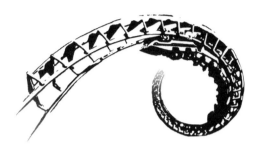

Chapter 2

GHOST TRAIN

"Is this it?" Gus asked Ricky. "This is your great idea?"

They were standing in front of the Ghost Train ride.

"Ghost Trains are for kids," Sam said. "They just ride by a few plastic skeletons and someone wearing a sheet. It's not scary."

"It's not exactly the Devil Dipper, is it?" Gus said.

"No, but it's our way of getting onto the Devil Dipper," Ricky told them.

Gus and Sam looked confused.

"It's dark in there," Ricky explained. "We hide until the park is closed. Then we get ourselves a free ride on the Dipper. Just jump off when I tell you."

Ricky went first. Small children were climbing onto the Ghost Train. The cars rattled into the tunnel.

Something flapped in Gus's face. It was a giant black bat. Screams rang out all around them.

A bony hand reached down in front of Sam. It didn't look like plastic.

Gus saw a huge spiderweb ahead.

His car was heading into it and a spider the size of a basketball was waiting.

Gus hated spiders.

He ducked his head and felt the sticky web pull at his hair.

Then suddenly Gus and Sam heard Ricky's voice. "Now!" Ricky whispered.

They all jumped, landing in a pile in the dark.

"That skeleton hand looked kind of real," Sam said.

"I didn't like the spiderweb, either," Gus said.

"Shh!" Ricky told them. "We need to be quiet."

Strange shadows danced on the walls. Weird noises rang out around them. There was an hour to wait before they could get out.

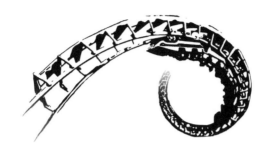

STEEL MONSTER

Finally, they heard the train rumble out of the tunnel. It was quiet.

"Let's wait for a little while," Ricky said. "They need time to close up the park. Then we can get out of here."

They waited for a few minutes, excited to ride on the roller coaster. Then the boys crept along the tunnel, past the skeletons and spiders that looked like floppy plastic now.

"I wasn't scared," Sam said. "The Ghost Train is for babies."

It was already dark outside. The park was empty.

"Okay!" Ricky said. "I saw what the guy did to start the Devil Dipper. Get on board and let's go!"

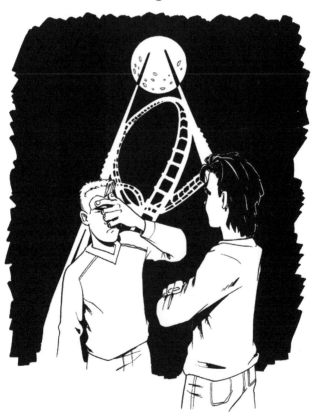

Gus and Sam were silent. They were looking up at the Devil Dipper. In the dark it looked more menacing. The twin spikes jabbed up at the sky.

"The seats flip backward when you start," Ricky told them. "We'll be looking up at the sky. Then at the top they flip forward so you're looking straight down!"

"Ricky, I'm not sure this is such a great idea," Gus said. "I mean, maybe it's not safe without someone at the controls."

"Are you scared or something?" Ricky asked. "I mean, the thing stops by itself."

"It does look sort of scary, with all the lights off and stuff," Sam said.

"You guys are babies," Ricky said with a mean laugh. "Well, if you want to miss out that's up to you. But I'm going to have the ride of my life."

Before Gus and Sam could stop him, Ricky had started the ride. Then he jumped on board and strapped himself into one of the seats.

"Bye!" Ricky shouted. Then the seat flipped backward and the train began its slow climb.

"Come on," Gus said to Sam. "There's no point in standing here. Let's go walk around."

When they looked back, Ricky's car had reached the top of the hill. It looked impossibly high. Then it swooped down and looped out of sight.

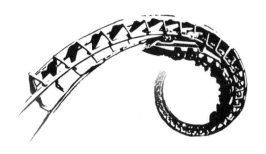

MISSING

"It's probably finished by now," Gus said. He and Sam headed back.

The ride was just slowing down. One by one, the cars clattered back along the tracks.

"Can't see him yet," Sam said. "Do you remember which car it was?"

"No," Gus said. "He was in the back, I think. He probably passed out from the gravity!"

They looked at each car as it came to the start of the ride.

Still no Ricky.

"Do you think he got off before we got here?" Sam said at last.

"Can't have," Gus said. "It was still moving, remember? Look, this is the end of the train. He must be in one of these cars."

One by one the cars came to a stop. Gus looked at Sam.

It didn't make sense. All of the seats were empty. There was no sign of Ricky anywhere.

"Check at the front again," Gus told Sam. "He's got to be somewhere."

"What if he fell out?" Sam asked.

"He was strapped in. He couldn't have," Gus said, feeling sick.

"Well, something happened," Sam said. "The only way we're going to find him is to get on the ride ourselves."

"No, Sam, I don't think we should," Gus said.

But it was too late.

Sam had started the thing up again. The train was climbing and Sam was on it.

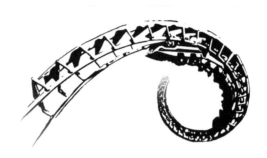

Chapter 5

ALONE IN THE PARK

Gus saw Sam's seat flip backward as the train climbed. "Awesome!" he heard Sam scream.

The clatter of the cars on the tracks seemed to get louder and louder as Sam reached the top of the hill. Then his car shot over the edge and swung into the huge loop of steel.

This time, Gus stood and waited. He would watch Sam's car, no matter what.

But the twisting maze of the Devil Dipper was almost too much to watch.

One minute the car was there, and then it shot out of sight.

Gus saw it climb one of the tall spikes. He heard Sam screaming. Then the car fell like a rocket out of the sky and Gus lost sight of it.

There was nothing to do but wait. The minutes seemed like hours.

Gus was beginning to feel sick again. He just wanted the ride to be over and for Ricky and Sam to be back. It was really dark and it was hard to see anything.

Finally, the wheel seemed to slow down. The cars began to clatter back, one by one. Gus counted them in. Another ten, and then it was Sam's.

Eight, nine, ten.

Gus stood in horror. The car was empty. Sam had disappeared, too.

Chapter 6

BACK IN THE TUNNEL

Gus didn't know what to do.

"Where are they?" he shouted, kicking one of the cars. The sound rang out around the park.

Then it was silent again. He was alone. Sam and Ricky had vanished into thin air.

They had to be somewhere. Gus began to search the park. He went to the arcade. It was empty.

Gus went back to the Ghost Train. It was closed for the night, but he found a way in. It was really dark and hard to see. Gus crawled along the tunnel.

Then suddenly he stopped. He heard a noise. It was someone whispering. His heart began to beat faster.

Skeletons and spiders were dancing in the shadows. Something brushed against his face, making him jump. But he had to keep going. He knew someone was in there.

He got closer, then stopped and listened. Someone spoke. "That skeleton hand looked kind of real."

It was Sam! That was exactly what he'd said when they'd been on the Ghost Train together.

"Ricky! Sam!" Gus shouted. But no one answered.

Then Gus heard something that made his blood run cold.

"I didn't like the spiderweb."

It was Gus's own voice. That was what he'd said before.

Chapter 7

NIGHT RIDE

Gus's head was spinning. The others were there.

In fact, they were all there, just as they had been earlier that day. But when he spoke, they didn't seem to hear him. It was like he wasn't there. Something was keeping them apart, like they were in two separate worlds.

His mind began to race. There was only one thing that was keeping him from his friends.

That was a ride on the Devil Dipper. Gus had a feeling that the only way he could get back to them was to go on the ride.

Slowly, he made his way over to the huge steel monster. His heart was racing as he started the thing up. He climbed on and strapped himself in.

Something told Gus this was going to be the ride of his life.

The car clattered slowly along the track. Then suddenly his seat swung backward and he was looking up at the stars. It felt like he was falling into the night sky.

It was a slow climb, and then the car stopped. He was hanging on the top of the hill.

Then his seat flipped forward and slid into the blackness.

Gus's hands went white as he held onto the rail in front of him. It felt like his head was coming off. The train was speeding into a double loop, but his seat was swinging around too, making him feel sick and dizzy.

The rollercoaster was getting faster and faster. It was out of control, rocketing through space.

Then suddenly there was a huge bang and lights flashed in Gus's face. The ride had crashed into the Amusement Arcade and was thundering past the machines.

Then there was another bang and it was dark again.

A white figure slid toward him, and Gus knew he was back in the Ghost Tunnel.

Chapter 8

REUNITED

Gus's head was still spinning, but he knew what he had to do.

He waited until he heard Sam say, "That skeleton hand was kind of real."

"I didn't like the spiderweb, either," Gus said.

"Shh!" Ricky told them. "We need to be quiet."

This was where it had to change.

"Sorry, guys," Gus said loudly.
"But we're getting out of here.
There's no way we're getting on that
thing again."

He scrambled to his feet, pushing
the others towards the exit.

Outside, it was still light.

Ricky and Sam looked confused.

"You said 'again,'" Ricky said. "You said, 'We're not getting on that thing again.'" He stared at Gus

"I think I sort of dreamed I was on it," Sam said, looking up at the Dipper.

Gus shook his head.

"No, guys. Don't you know what happened?" Gus said. "We've been on it. Don't you remember? It's not just a ride. It took us back in time."

They had reached the park gates. It was nearly closing time, and people were heading out of the park.

The three of them stood and looked back at the roller coaster.

"So it's like a time machine?" Ricky said. "Cool! I wonder how far back it can take you."

He waited a minute, until Gus and Sam were lost in the crowds.

Then he slipped back into the park.

ABOUT THE AUTHOR

Jillian Powell started writing when she was very young. She loved having a giant pad of paper and some pens or crayons in front of her. She made up newspaper stories about jewel thieves and spies. Jillian's parents still have her early stories, complete with crayon illustrations!

ABOUT THE ILLUSTRATOR

Paul Savage works in a design studio. He says illustrating books is "the best job." He's always been interested in illustrating books, and he loves reading. Paul also enjoys playing sports and running.

He lives in England with his wife and their daughter, Amelia.

GLOSSARY

accompanied (uh-KUM-puh-need)—not alone, with someone

arcade (ar-KADE)—an area with machines for amusement, like videogames and pinball

clatter (KLAT-ur)—bang together noisily

gravity (GRAV-uh-tee)—the force that pulls things down toward the Earth

menacing (MEN-iss-ing)—threatening or dangerous

rumbled (RUHM-buhld)—made a low, rolling noise like the sound of thunder

skeletons (SKEL-uh-tuhnz)—the bones that make up a body

strange (STRAYNJ)—different; odd, or peculiar

DISCUSSION QUESTIONS

1. Was it wrong for the boys to sneak onto the roller coaster after the park closed? Why or why not?

2. Are you afraid of any rides, like a roller coaster? What are the reasons you are or aren't?

3. Do you think time travel will ever be possible? If you could travel through time, where would you go?

WRITING PROMPTS

1. At the end of this book, Ricky sneaks back into the park. What happens next? Write a short story that tells what happens after Ricky leaves his friends.

2. Imagine that something in your house, town, or school is a secret time machine. What is it? Where would it take you? Describe your time machine and the adventure you go on.

3. What would have happened if Gus hadn't figured out how to stop the time travel? Write some things that might have happened.

OTHER BOOKS

The Reactor

When Joe and his friends are locked out of The Reactor, an abandoned building they have claimed as their own, they set out to uncover the sinister activities of those who inhabit the building.

Big Brother at School

The newly installed security cameras and the announcement of a special "health check" day have made Lee suspicious. He is determined to foil his principal's mysterious plan before it is too late!

BY J. POWELL

Sleepwalker

When Josh decides to follow Tom one night on one of his sleepwalking adventures, real life suddenly turns into a nightmare!

5010 Calling

The year is 5010. Beta sets up a thought-link with Zac, who lives in the year 2000 to help him with his history project. Then Beta gets Zac into trouble . . .

INTERNET SITES

Do you want to know more about subjects related to this book? Or are you interested in learning about other topics? Then check out FactHound, a fun, easy way to find Internet sites.

Our investigative staff has already sniffed out great sites for you!

Here's how to use FactHound:

1. Visit *www.facthound.com*

2. Select your grade level.

3. To learn more about subjects related to this book, type in the book's ISBN number: **1598898507**.

4. Click the **Fetch It** button.

FactHound will fetch the best Internet sites for you!